W9-CHZ-643

Put your name on things you don't want to lose.

This book belongs to

____

____

There are too many people to thank one by one, and I don't want to hurt anybody's feelings. So instead I want to say thank you to ALL of my family for always making sure I had lots of books and journals and encouraging me to read and write. Thank you, Mom, for always helping me with everything. You always make me the best dinners and take care of me. You always want me to be safe and teach me how to be good and safe even when I'm not with you. This is for you, Mom, to show you how much I listen to you and appreciate you and LOVE YOU!

♥ Isabella Thordsen

I dedicate this book to all of the friends and family who put a pencil and paper in front of me so I could write my thoughts.

♥ Isabelle Busath

And we would both like to thank Raymond Flores for abiding rule number 154 "Protect this rule book."

♥ Isabelle and Isabella

To my father, Ruben Garcia, gifted artist, whose view of life inspires me.

Priscilla Burris

Isabelle & Isabella's

Little Book of Rules

SIMON SPOTLIGHT
An imprint of Simon & Schuster Children's Publishing Division
1230 Avenue of the Americas, New York, New York 10020

Manufactured in the United States of America 0813 LAK
First Edition 2 4 6 8 10 9 7 5 3 1
ISBN 978-1-4424-9980-5
ISBN 978-1-4424-9981-2 (eBook)

Isabelle & Isabella's Little Book of Rules

by Isabelle Busath and Isabella Thordsen

illustrated by Priscilla Burris

SIMON SPOTLIGHT
New York London Toronto Sydney New Delhi

About this book . . .

Isabelle and Isabella are cousins. At the ages of ten and eight, they realized life would be so much simpler if it came with a little book of rules. (Haven't we all had that thought at one time or another?)

But Isabelle and Isabella took the thought one step further—since life doesn't come with a book of rules, why, they'd write one themselves. "If you obey the rules, you can have more fun," Isabelle explained.

The rule book started as a guide for Isabelle's younger sister, but it wasn't long before their list contained more than one hundred rules by which to live.

When the girls lost their precious rules book in a local store, they feared it was gone forever. But after a clerk found it and posted about it online, a national search was on to find the authors. Isabelle and Isabella became overnight sensations and made the rounds on the media circuit, sharing their wise rules with America.

We felt that their rules were, indeed, worth sharing. To that end, we've left Isabelle and Isabella's words pretty much exactly as written. Some of the rules are sweet, some are serious, and some are hilarious. They are a peek into Isabelle and Isabella's world, and what they decide is "rule worthy."

We hope you find them, as we do, rules worthy of living by.

Be nice to books.

1. No talking back.

2. No pushing.

3. No Screaming

4. Be Safe.

5. lisen

⑥ no being gross

⑦ Help others

⑧ care with others

⑨ no being bad

⑩ Have fun at All times.

I love to turn on my music in my room and dance.
Isabella

Don't chew
gum at school.

11. No lieing

12. No wineing

13. Be pawisitive

14. Be a good communicater

15. Be responsible

(16) Be Respectful

(17) Say sorry

(18) Say please

(19) Say thank you

(20) Have Good manners

(21) no yelling

(22) be nice to books.

(23) Ose good langvage.

(24) no teasing

(25) don't make fun of others.

(26) when sleeping don't wake others.

(27) Do what the parents ask you to do.

(28) Be unique

(29) Be your self

No being gross.

I mostly do dance. I run sometimes. But I don't play any sports.

(30) don't coppy others

(31) don't cheet on tests.

(32) study for tests_

(33) excercise

(34) Do things equaly with eachother.

(35) Do things yourself.

(36) Do your Homework.

(37) No Steeling

(38) No making unwanted noise.

Have fun
at all times.

Say sorry.
I'm sorry I called you Goofy.

(39) No saying ew when someone farts.

(40) Say excuse me.

(41) Don't color on people.

(42) Don't color on other peoples paper

(43) No spitting

(44) No squizing others.

(45) Try to complement.

(46) Don't Say no.

(47) Don't cry.

(48) no pulling hair.

(49) no turning your back.

(50) no punching

(51) no getting into others faces.

(52) no going under bed only if nessasary.

zzZ

Don't color on people.

53 Ceep your gum in your mouth.

54 No ruining bedding.

55 No coloring in rule book.

56 No jumping on bed.

Say "thank you."

No teasing.

57) No ignoring others.

58) No hiding from others.

59) No being loud.

60) Put your shoes by the front door when you take them off.

(61) ware enything yoo want.

(62) Keep dogs away from cats.

(63) don't call eachother names

(64) clean up your messes.

(65) no eating other peoples food.

(66) Go to bed at bed time.

(67) Do your Homework.

(68) Don't have a party without parents.

(69) If there is one bathroom. Go to the bathroom fast.

(70) Keep the envirment clean.

(71) Don't go running in the street or the parkin lot.

No
wasting paper.

Say "excuse me."

(72) Don't play with knifes.

(73) Have a parent guide you when cooking.

(74) Sit on your chair corectly.

(75) Drink water alot.

76 Don't touch Hot things unless with a parent.

77 Try to get good grades on tests.

78 Share

79 try to be a good big sister\brother

ABCDEFG

My favorite subject is writing, and my least favorite is math.

10
×25

35
- 17

Isabella

Don't color on
other people's paper.

(80) Stop at stop sighns and stop lights. (for parents) [rule written above "parents"]

(81) ware a seatbelt.

(82) pay attention in class.

(83) Don't steal

(84) wake up when ~~you~~ need to,

(85) Don't Get into other Peoples buisness.

(86) No running when it is slipperly

(87) always be polite

(88) no ditching.

(89) Go when you have to go.

(90) never leave a friend behind

No going under the bed,

only if it's necessary.

91 don't go running\walking in a basket bal court if someone is playing basketba

92 Ask permision

93 don't promis if your going to brake it

Think in a quiet place.

Don’t bite
the dentist.

(94) keep hands to yourself.

(95) Don't talk with your mouth full.

(96) Don't pick other people

(97) don't cat right lefope going to the dentist.

(98) Don't bite the dentist.

(99) Don't prive into road work.

(100) Don't suck your fingers

(101) Do your chores.

(102) Don't Text and Drive at the same tim.

(103) No toys at the table

(104) eat the food you got served with.

(105) Tie your shoes or you will fall.

(106) No elbows on the table

(107) Chew with your mouth closed

My favorite food is asparagus, and my least favorite food is chicken.
Isabelle

If there's one bathroom, go to the bathroom fast.

gg fgf gfccgfgcv

(108) don't eat when your mouth is numb

(109) No bribing

(110) Help new students

(111) Go through detector in stores.

(112) Try to make things fail.

(173) Don't talk to Strangers.

(114) Don't ask Quetions you don't want to know the Awnser to.

(115) Don't Go ontop of peple in pools.

(116) Keep your friends secerets.

(117) if ~~there's~~ there's no space between one person you want to sit by don't cry or wine because there is no room.

(118) Don't keep saying please if someone says, "no."

Keep your friend's secrets.

TOP SECRET Hat

(119) Don't eat your boogers from picking your nose.

(120) Don't sleep with your toys

(121) Don't keep other people awake after bed time.

I don't sleep with my toys. But I do sleep with stuffed animals and books under my pillows. My favorite is my monkey.
zzzzz
Isabella

Don't leave anybody out.

122 pay for everything you want to buye at thes stare.

123 Blow your nose not pick your nose.

124 Don't run in the house.

125 No hair pulling

(126) resicle

(127) no littering

(128) Don't be bossy.

(129) Don't play with your toys at night time.

(130) Don't talk peoples ears off

Tie your shoes,
or you will fall.

I usually wake up early in the morning, but I would like to sleep so I can see where my dreams lead me.
Isabelle

131 Read listen infrucktions

132 Go to bed early if you have dance in the moring

133 Don't stuff your mouth.

(134) let the dentists work in your mouth,

(135) let the doctor work on your body.

(136) worn others about danger. ~~around you~~.

(137) No cheating on other people

(138) Tell the teacher if your leaving.

(139) If you wet your bed, ware a pullup.

(140) Don't watch tv after bed time.

(141) don't chew gum at School

(142) don't chew gum if you ware brasses.

(143) No toys at School.

(144) Act in a mature way with self control and respect others.

Don't keep saying "please" if someone keeps saying "no."
Please
Please
Please
Please
Please

Don't sleep with your toys.

(145) don't ignor friends and parents,

(146) Don't get into peoples way if they are playing with a hoola hoop.

(147) Don't bounce on Hoola hoops.

(148) Don't skip Detention

(149) Don't skip school unless your sick.

(150) Keep your sleeves to your self.

(151) Keep your ~~self~~ feet and Shoes to your self.

(152) keep your Hair to your self.

(153) Ask if there ok.

(154) protect this rule book.

(155) protect each other.

(156) No toching other peoples body parts.

The best thing
about my family
is they always
help me.

Isabella

Don't get in people's way if they are playing with a Hula-Hoop.

(157) No poking

(158) no fake burping.

(159) no pinching

(160) no running in the halway at school.

(161) Be quit in the halway at school.

(162) No feet on the table.

(163) Don't wast paper.

(164) don't leave any body out

(165) No sneaking candy

(166) bring home all the homework you need to do.

(167) No wasting Paper.

(168) Think in a quit place

(169) If you Get a bad feeling about

Some one, don't trust them.

(170) look both ways before you cross the street,

(171) act your age.

(172) No breaking stuff.

Don't be selfish.

Be what you want to be.

I recycle cans and water bottles. And most everything else goes in the blue recycle bin.
RECYCLE
Isabella

(173) Don't be selfish.

(174) throw away your garbage

(175) don't eat like a pig.

(176) don't glare at people.

(177) Don't keep people waiting a long time.

(178) Smile infront of the camera

(179) don't throw food

(180) don't touch people and ditch them.

No sneaking candy.

Smile in front
of the camera.

(181.) No throwing anything.

(182) Don't laugh at people.

(183) No dogs on the conter.

(184.) don't bring your dog on the plane only if your blind.

185 no shooting people

186 don't teapla

187 no saying bad words any time.

188 dont jump off cliffs.

(189) No spying on people.

(190) don't poor water on people

(191) Don't play in Grampa's office.

(192) No pulling people.

(193) you need to be 8 to go in the front seat.

(194) no fighting when your mad.

If you see
someone sad,
ask if they're okay.

No whining.

NOOOOOOOOOOOO,
I don't
liiiiiike
Cuupcaaakessss!

(195) be good When you have a baby siter

(196) don't be picky.

(197) don't spit water at people.

(198) Don't do spit balls.

(199) When danctin
don't look for
parents.

(200) NO Smokeing.

(201) no stabbing
people

(202) no ding
dong ditching

I danced at a Rivercats baseball game recently, and I was distracted while looking for my parents. I kept messing up.
Isabelle

37 × 5 = 185
71 × 6 = 426
53 × 2 = 106

Keep your hair
to yourself.

Drink water a lot.

(203) No spraing on walls.

(204) don't do what your not soposet to do.

(205) Don't fart in peoples faces.

2

(206) Don't put your fingers in light sockets.

(207) Don't be in a field if there is no trees and there is lightning.

(208) no breaking into peoples houses.

(209) Don't go in your moms stuff

(210) don't be noisy back stage.

(211) Don't argue

(212) follow dilections

(213) wait for everyone to come out of the elevator before you go in.

No eating other people's food.

Put your name on things you don't want to lose.
Judy
Judy
Judy
Judy
Judy
Judy
Judy
Judy
Judy

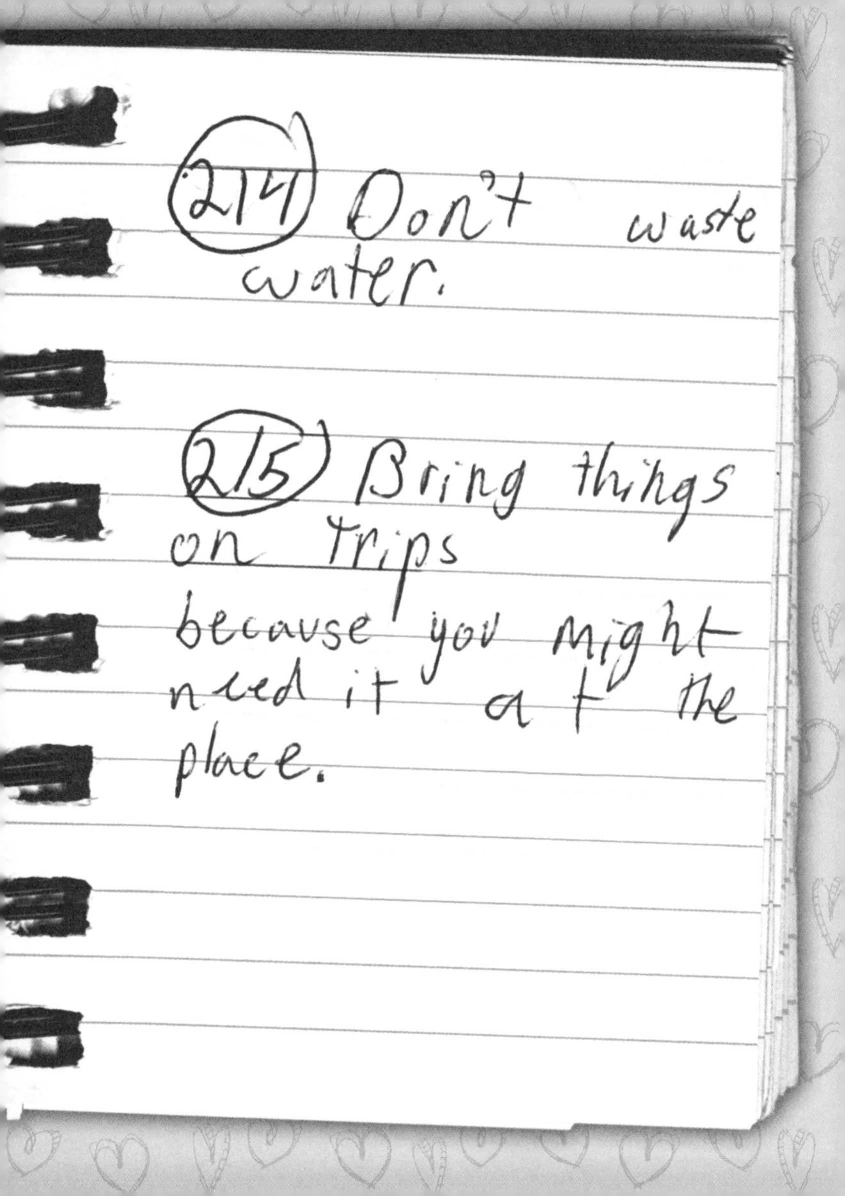
214 Don't waste water.
215 Bring things on Trips
because you might need it at the place.

(216) Be cheerful

(217) Be what you want to be

(218) put your name on things you don't want to lose.

Don't be bossy.

Wear anything you want.

Thank you for reading our book. We know it is hard to follow rules. We sometimes have a hard time following them ourselves! We worked hard on our rules. When we wrote our book, we didn't think anyone would ever read them but us! We wrote down rules that were special and mattered to us. When we found out we were getting a real book that everyone was going to read, we wanted to make sure that we left blank pages in case anyone wanted to add rules to the book that were special to them. If you want to, please use these blank pages to write down any extra rules that mean a lot to you.

We would like to thank Simon & Schuster, with special acknowledgment to Lisa Rao, Valerie Garfield, and Chani Yammer for their hard work and for seeing the potential of this book. We would also like to thank Barbara Moulton, of The Moulton Agency, for the effort and dedication to this project. Without her, we would have gone crazy. Finally, thank you to Priscilla Burris. Your artwork conveys the feel of the book in a manner that truly captures the spirit of the rules and our girls!

Sarah Tatarakis
Isabella Thordsen
Michelle Busath
Isabelle Busath

protect
each other.